THE
Balmaha
Bears

The Legend

Text © Keith and Carole Meara
Illustrations © David Carpenter

First Published in 2003 by:
Glowworm Books Ltd, Unit 7, Greendykes Industrial Estate,
Broxburn, West Lothian, EH52 6PG, Scotland.

Telephone: 01506-857570
Fax: 01506-858100

URL: http://www.glowwormbooks.co.uk

ISBN 1 871512 68 9

Printed and bound in Scotland

Designed by Caleb Rutherford eidetic
Edited by Lindsey Fraser

Reprint Code   10   9   8   7   6   5   4   3   2   1

THE Balmaha Bears

Keith and Carole Meara

Illustrations by David Carpenter

The Balmaha Bears loved stories. The children's favourite was The Legend, the story of the Balmaha Bears and how they came to live in their big underground cave. The best storyteller was Fraser Bear, the Innkeeper, the oldest and wisest bear.

"Long, long ago, our ancestors were huge brown bears who lived in caves around Loch Lomond. They ate sweet berries in autumn and ripe fruit in summer, they caught fat fish in the loch and collected sticky honey from the bees. All bears love honey, don't they?"

The little bears rubbed their tummies and licked their lips.

"One year the weather was terrible and every year after that it became worse. The lochs, rivers and streams froze over and deep snow covered the bears' favourite bushes. They couldn't find enough food and their stores of nuts and berries were running very low. How would they survive?"

"But things were even worse than that. Human beings who lived nearby were cold and hungry too, and some of them hunted the bears so that they could keep themselves warm with their thick, warm, furry coats."

The little bears gasped in horror and clung tightly to each other at the very idea of being hunted and losing their fur.

"The bears who escaped hid in caves near here at Balmaha. As the years went by, they went deeper and deeper under the mountains, living quietly and safely on roots, mosses and small herbs that they found. The cave roofs got lower and lower and, over time, the bears became smaller, until they were the size we are now".

"But how did they find this special cave?" asked a little bear.

"Graham Bear found it. He was
a great explorer, and when he told the
others about this magical place, with running water,
buzzing bees and singing birds, they couldn't wait to see it."

"Buchanan Bear, the Builder, said it was just the place to build
houses and he asked MacKay Bear, the Carpenter, to help. Before long,
they all moved into their new homes. There were trees,
berry bushes, lots of plants nearby and a stream with
trout and salmon. Some of the bears found little
tufts of wool and made soft beds for everyone.
They'd been dropped by the birds who
nested in the roof of our cave.
It was perfect!"

"But where did the light come from, Fraser Bear?" asked a little voice.

"Light came from the same white quartz Daylight Stone we know today. We still don't know how, but it seems to trap sunshine from those little gaps in the roof, the spaces the birds and bees use to fly in and out. Then the Daylight Stone shines for all it's worth. What would we do without it?"

The little bears sighed, they couldn't imagine living in darkness.
"But what did they do next?" they asked.

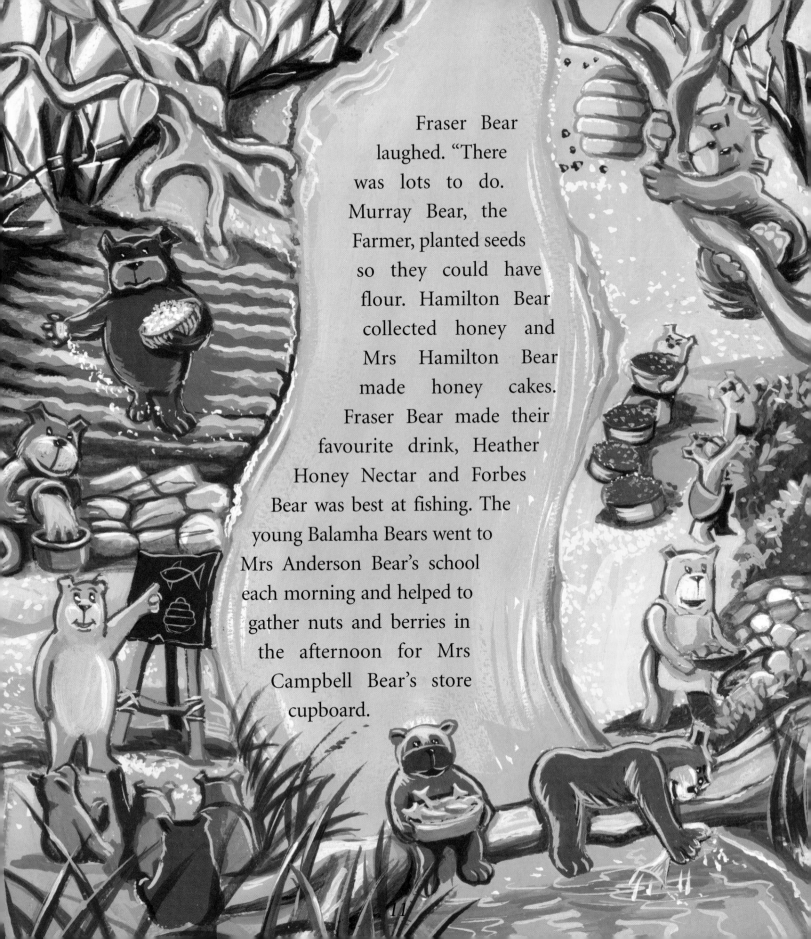

Fraser Bear laughed. "There was lots to do. Murray Bear, the Farmer, planted seeds so they could have flour. Hamilton Bear collected honey and Mrs Hamilton Bear made honey cakes. Fraser Bear made their favourite drink, Heather Honey Nectar and Forbes Bear was best at fishing. The young Balamha Bears went to Mrs Anderson Bear's school each morning and helped to gather nuts and berries in the afternoon for Mrs Campbell Bear's store cupboard.

"Where did our clothes come from?"
asked another small bear.

"That was Mrs MacDonald Bear's idea. Some of the older bears couldn't always tell who was who, so she designed special tartans for each family. She used berry juices, mosses and crushed brightly coloured pebbles to make the colours and dyed lots of wool. Then MacKay Bear made a loom and they wove the cloth. MacKenzie Bear, the Tailor, made the scarves and tammies. That's why we all have different tartans. We're all Balmaha Bears, but we're all just that wee bit different."

Fraser Bear always ended his
story like that. The young bears
clapped their paws and growled happily.
They'd heard it again and again, and they
loved it every time.

"Now, here are your mums and dads to take
you home for tea. Off you go!"

One little bear was missing. Mrs MacDonald
Bear was frantic. "Baby MacDonald must
have gone off on his own," said the others.
"He was definitely here at the start!"

The search was on.

"I've found his tammy!" yelled MacFarlane Bear, and everybody rushed towards him.

"Quiet!" he ordered. "I'm sure I can hear something." Silence fell and sure enough they could hear faint baby-bear cries coming from beyond the cave wall.

"How did he get in there?" asked an astonished MacKay Bear. "There must be an opening somewhere."

They searched frantically. At last Buchanan Bear shouted, "Here's an opening but it's far too small for any of us to get through."

"Let's get digging, and hurry," said Fraser Bear, and they set to…

They dug, and dug and the young bears hauled the stones away from the hole.The cries were getting louder as the hole got bigger.

"Let me try and get through," said Miss MacLean Bear. "I'm the skinniest bear!"

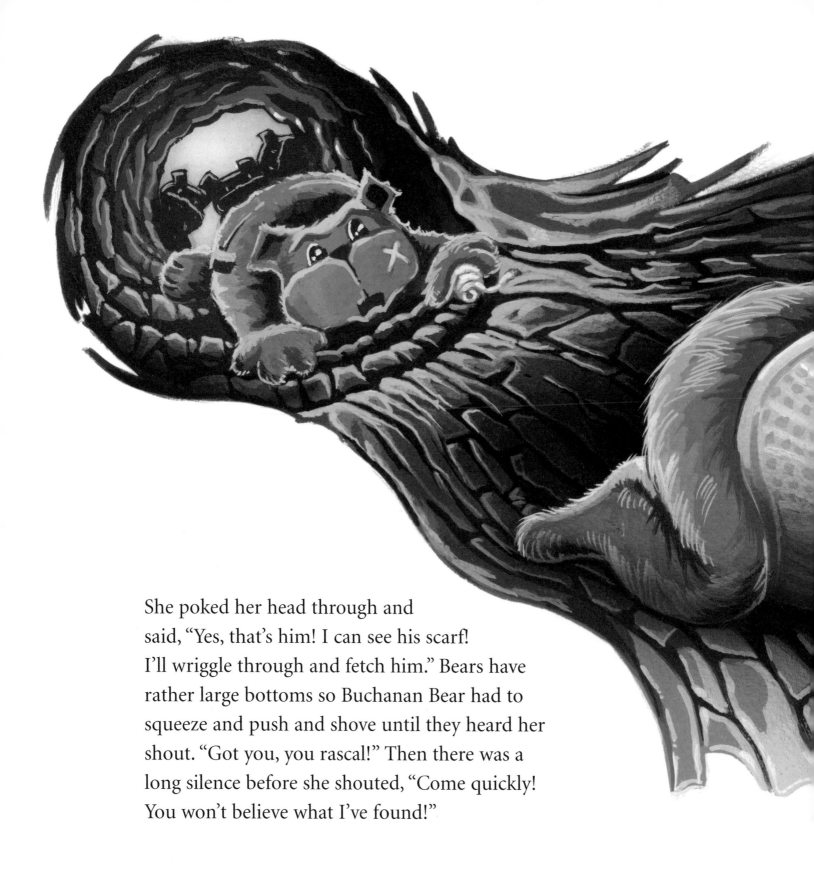

She poked her head through and
said, "Yes, that's him! I can see his scarf!
I'll wriggle through and fetch him." Bears have
rather large bottoms so Buchanan Bear had to
squeeze and push and shove until they heard her
shout. "Got you, you rascal!" Then there was a
long silence before she shouted, "Come quickly!
You won't believe what I've found!"

The rest of the Balmaha Bears clawed at the opening and, after a few minutes, they followed Miss MacLean Bear into the new tunnel and saw what she and Baby MacDonald had discovered.

It was a beautiful new world.

There were tall leafy trees, a white sandy beach, green grass and dancing clear blue water. Beyond the water there were purple and green mounds - Miss MacLean Bear said they must be the hills she remembered her grandmother telling her about.

But on top
of it all, like the icing
on a cake, was a beautiful
blue sky, with little fluffy white
clouds. All the bears looked up in
astonishment. They'd heard all about the
sky from their stories, but they had never
imagined it could look so fabulous.

None of them said a word until Dr Graham Bear appeared and demanded to see Baby MacDonald. "He could have hurt himself, for all I know. I must take him back at once and give him a check-up. You can never be to careful," she told them. She took Baby MacDonald by the paw and led him back through the passage, saying, "I don't know… You could have been badly hurt creeping away like that…" as she went. The rest of the bears followed slowly, pleased to have found the baby, but quite bewildered by what they'd seen.

Next morning, the Balmaha
Bears decided that they ought to
explore this magical new cave. They
chose three of the bravest bears for
the trip and, not long after breakfast,
MacMillan, MacKay and MacFarlane
Bears set off, promising to return
before nightfall.

21

Some of the older bears were just beginning to worry, when the three explorers returned. As Dr Graham Bear put wild garlic poultices on their scrapes and bruises, they explained that they'd walked all day, but never reached the edge of the cave.

"We don't think it's a cave," said MacFarlane Bear.

"There was water all around us," added MacKay Bear.

"So we think we're on an Island," cried MacMillan Bear. "We think
it's the place where our ancestors lived." There was a wee silence
as the Balmaha bears remembered what had happened to some
of those big bears. Without another word, they all moved
forward and blocked up the new tunnel opening.

"Can't be to careful," said
Fraser Bear quietly.

The next day, MacKay, MacMillan and MacFarlane Bears set off again. They scrambled through the rocky tunnel and came out into their magical new land, just as they had the day before. They whistled and hummed happily as they walked. After all, what could they possibly have to be afraid of?

Then they saw it!

24

It was a huge
four-legged, brown,
furry monster, which stopped
only to pull leaves from the
branches of the trees beside the path.

The bears froze, but when it saw them the
monster said, "Hello there," in a remarkably
friendly voice. "You look a bit like the huge
brown bears I've heard about from my mum and
dad, but you're absolutely tiny! Who are you?"

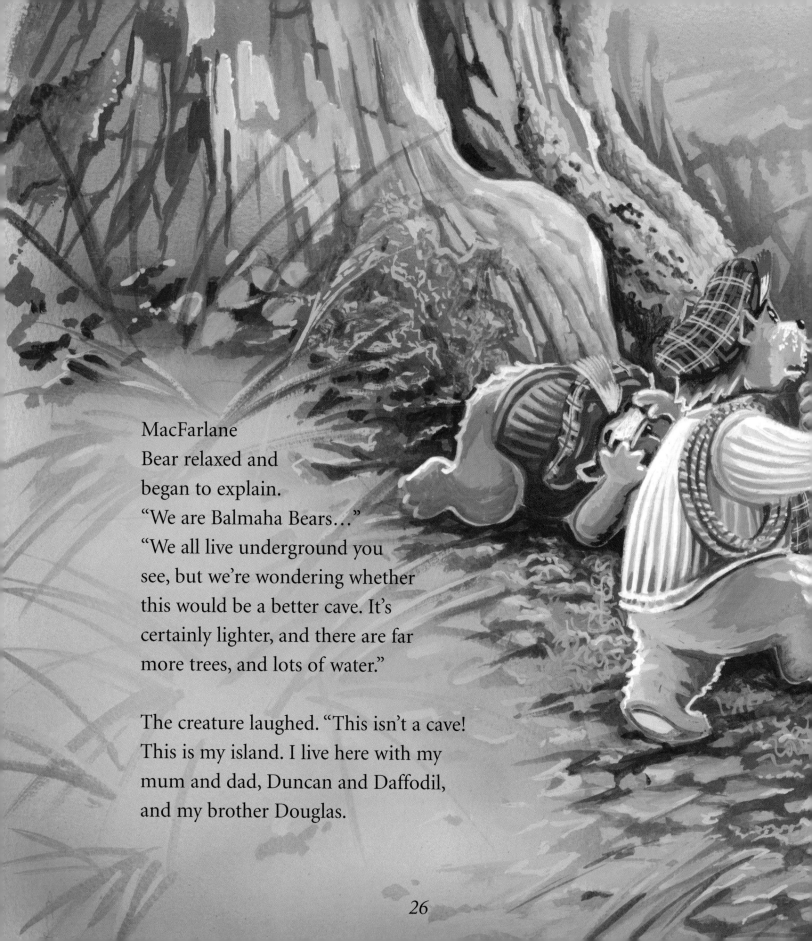

MacFarlane
Bear relaxed and
began to explain.
"We are Balmaha Bears…"
"We all live underground you
see, but we're wondering whether
this would be a better cave. It's
certainly lighter, and there are far
more trees, and lots of water."

The creature laughed. "This isn't a cave!
This is my island. I live here with my
mum and dad, Duncan and Daffodil,
and my brother Douglas.

My name's
Daisy, by the way.
All our names begin
with D because that goes
best with Deer."

"Ahh," said MacFarlane Bear,
looking very pleased with himself,
"you're not a monster, you're a deer.
I've heard all about you from Fraser
Bear. You don't eat bears." All three
Balmaha Bears looked
very relieved indeed!

27

"Of course not!" laughed Daisy. "Now come and meet my family,"
and she trotted off towards the shore with the bears in hot
pursuit. Their legs were so much shorter than Daisy's that by
the time they reached the other deer, they were
terribly out of breath.

"Welcome to Inchcailleach Island," said Duncan, once they'd been introduced. "Humans come here from time to time, but Angus, the warden protects all the animals. You'll be safe here if you decide to leave your underground caves. They'll always be there if you need them. Go back to your families and tell them that the Deer Family would be delighted to welcome new neighbours."

The three explorers couldn't wait to get back to their cave
to tell everybody what they'd seen and whom they'd met.

"You should see it, it's fantastic!" said MacMillan Bear.

"It's brilliant," said MacFarlane Bear.

"It's cool," said MacKay Bear.

"Not too cool, I hope," said Fraser Bear quietly.
"That's how the trouble started."

They told the others
that Inchcailleach was
the loveliest place they'd
ever seen, and that the Deer
Family had promised to help
them set up new homes, in caves
right at the top of the island. "Are you
sure it's safe?" demanded Mrs Fraser Bear,
"I'm not going anywhere we could be hunted".

"All right, all right," smiled Fraser Bear. "We'll all go tomorrow to see this wonderful place and, if everybody is happy with what we find, we'll head for those caves and a new life for the Balmaha Bears."

"After all, I think its high time that I had a new story to tell," he added, ruffling the ears of the young bears sitting next to him. "I wonder just what that will be all about?"